GW00890078

The Willy Enlarging Elixir

Contains rude words

and other stories

Crazy Horse Press
116, Bewdley Road, Stourport,
Worcs DY13 8XH
Tel: 01299 824858
email: phayden@crazyhpress.demon.co.uk
website: www.crazyhpress.demon.co.uk

© Peter Hayden 1999
illustrations © Clinton Banbury 1999
ISBN 1 871870 10 0

This book is sold subject to the condition that it shall not, by way of trade or otherwise, be lent, resold, hired out or otherwise circulated without the publisher's prior consent in any form of binding or cover other than that in which it is published and without a similar condition being imposed on the subsequent publisher.

Printed by T. Snape & Co Ltd., Boltons Court, Preston PR1 3TY. Tel: 01772 254553 Fax: 01772 204697

About This Book

The Stringy Simon stories are a collection of 45 linked short-stories taking a young boy through the highs and lows of his junior school years.

1	Stewart Makes a Potion	2	The Big Catch
3	Portly Paul Buys a Bed	4	The Hole in the Bucket
5	The Sneeze	6	Fish-finger Day
7	The Holiday	8	The Off-white House
9	Rocky's Little Game	10	Stewart and the Cavity
11	The Auction	11½	The Incredible Dream
12	The Famous Tasting Ceremony	13	The Mothers' Day Card
14	Mr Smart Gets a Shock	15	The Old People's Party
16	Stewart Starts a Diet	17	Mr Whippy's Boo-boo
18	The Fabulous Koala Bear	19	The Long Wash
20	Stewart and the Spitfire	21	Curlie Makes a Hit
22	Doctor Rawalpindi	23	Stewart and the Briar Patch
24	The Last Sparkler	25	Stewart Learns to Swim
26	The Conker Champion	27	Mr Toad Finds a Pond
28	An Aussie Invite	29	Stewart's Chrissie Surprise
30	Stewart Makes It Big	31	Stewart and the Cicadas
32	Froggy's Little Mistake	33	Douglas the Dogless
34	Accrington Stanley Win the Cup	35	Portly Paul Saves the Day
36	Batty Goes Shopping	37	Stewart and the Forest Creature
38	A True Scotsman	39	Jurgen Gets a Fright
40	Mme Murgatroyd's Secret Nest	41	The Swiss Army Knife
42	Stewart and the Burglars	43	The Very Special Sample
44	Stewart makes His Mark	45	The Willy Enlarging Elixir

"The Willy Enlarging Elixir" contains stories 2, 21, 26, 29, 40 and 45.

Stories 1, 16, 20, 25, 27, 31 and 34 can be found in "The Adventures of Stringy Simon".

The third title in the series, called "The Sneeze & Other Stories", is available from spring 2000. It begins at the beginning, and tells the first seven stories in sequence.

Look out for further titles bringing you all the Stringy Simon stories in their proper order.

For details see back page order form.

THE BIG CATCH

[It's the day after Stewart, Stringy Simon's son, has nearly landed him in serious trouble by mixing a demon potion in a bottle of wine which he accidentally gave to his huge friend, Portly Paul...]

It was still lovely and sunny the next day, the day after the serious incident with the wine, and Stringy Simon decided to go for a walk in the park and feed the ducks. Whenever they bought a loaf of bread, Stringy Simon and Patsy would feed the loaf to the ducks and save the crumbs for themselves. Down past the park there was a stream which ran through the meadows for miles and miles until it was out of sight, and on the bank of that stream, gazing quietly out by himself, was a fisherman. He was always there. He had a little folding stool, a tin of maggots that wriggled and writhed all day, a thermos flask of hot coffee with brandy in it to warm his insides, and a long green landing net. But he never caught anything. He would throw handfuls of maggots into the water to tempt the fish to his line. But the fish were bored with maggots. They'd been living off fishermen's maggots for years, it was giving them indigestion. They wanted a change.

The maggots quite enjoyed their little dip. They especially liked whizzing through the air when they were thrown in and would let out teeny little squeals of delight that are *inaudible* to the human ear. The fish would hear them though. 'Look out lads,' the oldest one would say. He was a miserable old carp who'd been flushed down the loo years before when his owners had decided to fill in the garden pond and put a whirly-round washing line there instead. He still remembered the good old days of dried fish food with pink and yellow flakes. 'Look out,' he'd say to the other fish, 'here comes trouble,' and the next minute dozens of squealing giggling maggots would hit the water with a splash and start racing each other to the opposite bank.

Stringy Simon didn't go near the river cause he couldn't swim. He was afraid someone would mistake him for a fishing rod and thread a maggot onto his nose. He didn't go too near the duck pond in the park either. He would sit on a bench and the ducks would come waddling up to him for their bread, and when they'd had enough they'd waddle back again.

Portly Paul liked the park, because he could get up to *mischief* there. He would bang his belly against the big horse chestnut trees and make all the conkers fall down. He would put sticks in the crazy golf so people's shots would keep coming back to them. He would let the brakes off prams while mums were feeding their babies.

But the thing he liked best was interfering with the signs. By scratching bits off and adding bits on he could change the words. If it said 'District Council' at the bottom he would change it to 'Dirty Scoundrel'. If it said 'Town Clerk', he would change it to 'Brown Nerk'. One sign said, 'Dogs must be kept on a lead', and after lots of careful scratching and altering he changed it to 'Poos must be left on a seat'.

Behind Stringy Simon's bench was a big clump of bushes. Portly Paul strolled down the foot-path with his felt pen and scraper in his pocket, looking for mischief. He saw the ducks and thought, 'Ah-ha, I'll hide behind the bushes and give them a fright.' But the ducks heard him crushing sticks and twigs and waddled back to the water. When he jumped out to scare them they were gone. Only Stringy Simon was there.

'So! It's *you* is it,' Portly Paul thundered, 'the one who wizzed in the wine. I'll make you pay you rotten sliver of skin and bone, you won't get away from me this time.'

He came round the front of the bench with his arms out, blocking out the sun and making it impossible for Stringy Simon to get past. He moved towards him menacingly, but just as he was about to squash the living daylights out of him, Stringy Simon turned sideways, lay flat along the bench and rolled between the gaps. Then he nipped into the bushes behind and disguised himself as a stick.

Portly Paul was furious. He trampled in after him but couldn't find him. The parky was doing a slow tour of inspection on his bike when he heard the crack of busting branches and sped over to investigate.

'Oi, get out of there you little pest,' he yelled, 'before I twist your ear off.'

It was too much for Stringy Simon. He thought Portly Paul must have a gang with him. He bolted for the railings. Portly Paul gave out a blood-curling howl of vengeance and went after him, leaving bits of bush scattered everywhere. Once he was out in the open the parky realised he was quite a *big* pest, but that didn't put him off.

'Come back here you little pair of beggars,' he yelled, pedalling after them for all he was worth.

Stringy Simon reached the railings first and slipped through the gap to safety. Portly Paul didn't have time to slow down before he thudded into them. They bent outwards a bit, and sent him whanging backwards. The parky went full tilt into him and came off his bike. Lucky for him he did, cause Portly Paul stepped back onto the wheel making the spokes ping like piano strings, and then fell backwards across the frame, buckling it completely.

Now that he was quite safe Stringy Simon could afford to have a good laugh. He looked at the two dazed and spluttering figures the other side of the railings and laughed like a drain. In fact he laughed so much he fell *down* a drain. He was so busy laughing as he walked away that he forgot to check where he was about to cross. Most people stop and check for cars first before they step into the road, but Stringy Simon was so thin he always had to check for *drains* first then cars second. And this time he was laughing so much he stepped straight off the kerb and down between a drain grating.

A tiny cry disappeared downwards, followed by a wincy splash, and then nothing. Silence.

Portly Paul and the parky helped each other up and charged round to the gate and back where the drain was. They stared down into the dark water for a long time but there was nothing to be seen or heard. After a while they shrugged their shoulders. What was there to do but pack up and go home? Even though the parky's bike was smashed to pieces he said nothing. It seemed wrong to make a fuss over a bike when he'd just seen a grown man disappear for ever.

* * * * *

Along by the stream the fisherman was ready to pack up and go home too. He hadn't caught a fish all day of course and he was beginning to get chilly. As he wound his line in for the last time he felt a strong tug. He leapt off his stool and wound in for all he was worth. 'I've got something!' he shouted to nobody, 'I've got a blinking fish at last!' The rod was bent double he reeled in so fast. It was a long thin fish he could tell as he caught a glimpse of it coming towards the surface. Probably an eel.

'An eel,' he yelled at the top of his voice, 'I've caught one, a damn great river eel!' It wasn't wriggling like an eel though, it was quite limp and still. He slipped his long green landing net under it and hauled it in. It was Stringy Simon.

'Oh my God, I've caught a bloke,' he said, unhooking his jacket collar. He tipped him upside down and shook him till all the water came out. Then he held him by the nose and poured coffee and brandy in his mouth. It was no good. He had to be getting home for his tea, so he hung Stringy Simon over the branch of a tree to dry while he collected his things together. He threw the last of the maggots into the water and unscrewed the sections of his rod. He was nearly ready. He looked at Stringy Simon draped motionless over the tree. 'I can't just leave him there,' he thought, 'it wouldn't be right. Someone must own him.' Then he had an idea. He slid Stringy Simon into his rod case and did up the buckle. He fitted exactly. He slung him over his shoulder, picked up the rest of his tackle and started on his way home. 'I'll drop him off at casualty,' he thought. 'They'll probably want to run a couple of tests on him.'

As he was walking along, the fisherman thought he felt a slight movement from his fishing rod case, and he stopped to tighten the strap. Then there was another movement, more of a twitch, and then there was a wriggling and a fidgeting.

'Oh have mercy on me,' came a muffled voice from inside the case, 'I beg forgiveness.'

The shocked fisherman took the rod case off his shoulder and tried to prop it against a wall to undo it, but it stood on end by itself. He loosened the buckle and flipped it open.

Stringy Simon blinked in the sunlight.

'Are you the devil?' he said.

'No,' said the puzzled fisherman, 'I'm Fred Cartwright and I fished you out of the river. What's all this devil malarky then?'

Stringy Simon climbed out of the case. He was a bit wobbly but apart from that he seemed alright. 'It was so hot and dark in there,' he said, 'I thought I must have drowned and gone straight down to hell.'

'That's not hell, that's my fishing rod case,' said Fred. 'Lucky for you it was warm, that's probably what revived you and got your circulation going. Well, at least you've saved me a journey. I can get straight off home now. Cheerio then. Watch where you're going next time.'

'Bye,' said Stringy Simon. 'Thank you for fishing me out.'

'Hmm,' he thought as he made his way home, 'that fishing rod case would make a jolly nice sleeping bag. I must see if I can get one.'

* * * * *

Fred got home just as his wife was pouring the tea.

'Did you catch anything then?' she said. She always asked, just to be polite.

'Yes,' said Fred, 'I did.'

‘Ooh!’ said his wife, nearly dropping her plate in surprise. ‘Where is it? Let’s have a look then.’

Fred took a slurp of his tea and a bite of banana sandwich.

‘It was only a tiddler,’ he said. ‘So I let it go.’

CURLIE MAKES A HIT

[After Stewart nearly destroys the Imperial War Museum on their trip to London, Stringy Simon and Patsy decide to take him somewhere nice and safe.]

It was Stringy Simon, Patsy and Stewart's last night in London, and after all their disasters they decided it would be best to take Stewart somewhere where he couldn't wander off. And it was Patsy who came up with the idea that they could go round to *Television Centre* and queue up and see if they could get tickets for one of the programmes.

There was quite a big queue when they got there, most of them with a coach party down from Wales for the day.

After a while, a rather smart B.B.C. man with a bow-tie came into the foyer and said, 'Tickets for "Doctor in the *Hise*" now available....'

'Over yer mun,' called the party leader, a roly-poly man who looked a bit like the large one from Little and Large, 'we'll take a fyew....'

They milled happily around the B.B.C. man until he gave up trying to boss them into line and dished out all the tickets.

'D'yeu think you could sign my carryer-bag? I've never spoken to a *pro*-per T.V. star before. Isn't it exciten'.'

'Come on Gwyneth, or we won't have time for the Houses of Parlyament.'

'Comen' Dai.'

The last member of the party scurried through the double doors with her bowler hat and signed Carnaby Street carrier-bag.

Stringy Simon, Patsy and Stewart waited patiently for their turn.

The B.B.C. man frowned at them. 'Aren't you going to join your *chums* at the Hise of Commons,' he said, trying to sound dignified again.

'Oh, no,' said Stringy Simon, 'we're on our own. It's our last night in London.'

'Oh *dyah*....' the man said, to himself, 'I seem to have given all the tickets *ite* I'm afraid.' He looked at their faces. 'Mmm. I *might* be able to find you something. Just hang on there a mo would you?'

He went off, and came back with some more tickets.

'Doctor in the Hise is absolutely *chockers* I'm afraid,' he said. 'High abite Top of the Pops? Would that *suit* you?'

Stewart looked up at them.

'Please...'

Stringy Simon bit his bottom lip hard, and took the tickets.

* * * * *

Now Stewart didn't have too much in the way of smart gear. He had his white jacket and trousers, which he called his Milky Bar Kid kit, or a pair of ordinary jeans which you might call *drainpipes*, or in Stewart's case *drinking-straws*, and a jumper. He went for the Milky Bar Kid kit, and sneaked a squirt of his mum's setting lotion to see if he could spike his hair up a bit. Even so, he didn't look too crucial, if you know what I mean, except compared to Stringy Simon and Patsy. And they looked so uncrucial you could have been forgiven for thinking they were off to the Co-op for the weekly shop, instead of a live showing of Top of the Pops at the B.B.C. studios.

But fortunately for Stewart, when they got in the lights were so bright and the bands were so loud that Stringy Simon and Patsy decided to go off to the canteen and sample the famous B.B.C. tea instead.

'Don't wander off....' shouted Stringy Simon over the din.

'And don't touch anything,' added Patsy.

And off they went.

* * * * *

Now Stewart's favourite singer at that time was Curlie Maguire. And as he wasn't a very good dancer - in fact he couldn't dance his way out of a *wet paper bag* - he decided to slip between all the other people and make his way up to the gallery where Curlie would be singing, so he would be sure of a place at the front. Of course, being number one in the charts meant that her spot would be last on the show, and Stewart passed the time watching the fabulous dancers, with their brilliant clothes and hairstyles, wishing he could be like them.

At last it was Curlie's turn.

She seemed small, and full of *vitality* in her fantastic yellow jump-suit, and all the fans, including Stewart, leaned forward as far as they could to get a clear view of her. As Stewart was straining forward, he felt a kind of slight tickle from his ear, and Curlie's voice came rushing in clearer than ever.

One of his grommets had fallen out.

Now Stewart had never actually seen a grommet because he'd been put to sleep, or *anaesthetised*, when the doctors had inserted them, and he was rather curious. He leaned over as far as he possibly could, and there, on the stage, like a tiny bead, there it was.

Curlie was still singing at the top of her voice and dancing about the stage. She was dancing to one side and then to the other, then to the front and then the back, so all the fans would get a chance to see her close to, and as she came towards the gallery she noticed Stewart leaning out towards the stage, and went towards him thinking he was an especially dedicated fan.

Still singing she stretched her hand out for him to touch.

'Look out!' yelled Stewart. And the next minute he was over. Curlie was over too. She'd stepped on the grommet and it had shot out from under her like a marble and left her sprawling on the floor. Stewart came down with a thump, on top of her.

* * * * *

Down in the B.B.C. canteen, there was a *monitor*, so people could still see the show while they were eating.

There was Curlie Maguire, dancing over towards the gallery.

Patsy stopped in mid-gulp. 'Look, it's Stewart,' she gasped, 'leaning over the gallery. He'll fall off if he's not....'

'Where?' said Stringy Simon.

But he was too late. On the monitor, and on all the screens in the sitting rooms up and down Britain, there was a quick review of the Top Ten, and then the D.J. was telling who would be on the following week. They had managed to cut the shot in time.

'Too late,' said Patsy, finishing her tea, 'you missed him.'

* * * * *

Back on the set it was bedlam, and it was two or three minutes before they could get to Stewart and Curlie and carry them off back-stage.

'What the devil do you think you were up to,' shouted the producer, who had dashed down from his box as soon as they'd got the show off the air.

Almost in tears, Stewart explained about the grommet and how he'd tried to warn Curlie but the music had drowned his voice.

The producer was not very impressed. But before he could find enough nasty words to give Stewart the telling-off of his life, Curlie stepped in.

'Leave'um alone, ya great Pommy *galah*,' she said. 'How'ud you like ut if someone started yelling at *you* after you'd jest had a hair-raisin' fall. You lay off hum...' She went and sat next to him, and took his hand. 'Are y'alright now mate?'

Stewart nodded his head but couldn't speak. Curlie Maguire was holding his hand. He thought he might be in a coma.

The producer fumed and clutched his clipboard. He wasn't allowed to argue with the stars.

'Very well,' he said, 'but don't let me see you again. Now off you go.'

As Stewart stood up Curlie gave him a wink.

'Don't take any notice of *hum*,' she said. 'You come beck any time ya want. An if you have any trouble getting in, tell um to come an fetch me.'

She glared at the producer to make sure he didn't *contradict* her, gave Stewart's hand a little squeeze, and placed a kiss gently on his cheek.

* * * * *

'You were on the T.V.,' said Patsy excitedly in the taxi home, 'we saw you on the monitor, just for a split second, leaning right out from the gallery. Bit risky wasn't it,' she added, 'what would you have done if you'd fallen?'

'Don't know,' said Stewart. He told them about the missing grommet, but *not* what had happened after he'd lost it. 'At least I managed to see what one looks like,' he said.

'Must be your lucky day then,' said Patsy. 'And you got right near the front for that little Cutie Whateverhernameis. I bet you were almost touching her.'

'Yes', said Stewart, with a sigh of pleasure. 'I suppose I must have been.'

THE CONKER CHAMPION

[Stewart and his folks were sort of persuaded to buy a shop after their caravan crashed into it. It starts off as an ice-cream parlour, but then becomes a toy hospital - a place for fixing up and recycling busted toys.]

I don't know if I mentioned this before, but there were two schools in the town where Stewart lived: Down-By-The-Traffic-Lights School which had churchey windows and a wicket painted on the wall, and Halfway-Up-The-Hill School which had a lobby with a coffee table, and a playing field. Stewart had started going to Halfway-Up-The-Hill School when they lived in their caravan, and it was halfway *down* the hill for him to get there. In fact they had passed it, very fast, the time they all crashed through the window of Patsy's Parlour. And when they finally moved in he decided to stay there - even though they were now nearer to Down-By-The-Traffic-Lights School - with Sam the hamster and Mrs Hodgetts. And Lucy Baggage.

At home-time the kids from the two schools would meet in the park and push each other off the swings and have 'anyway' contests - anyway we don't have to sing in assembly, anyway our teacher's got a new car, anyway we're going out in a coach - but underneath they always knew that schools are the same everywhere, they let you out at quarter to four and then you can get on with the serious business of playing.

Now that Patsy's Parlour had become a toy hospital, whenever a new consignment of broken toys appeared the grown-ups always let Stewart have a little *rummage* first to see if he would spot anything precious.

One day Stewart was busy rummaging through a box of particularly old junk which the adults had left untouched ready for him, when down in the bottom corner his busy fingers happened to touch upon two hard round pebbly knobbly shapes.

And what do you think the hard round pebbly knobbly shapes were, lying down there in the bottom of the box of junk and broken toys?

Yes, you've got it, they were the ends of Portly Paul's fingers which he had pushed through the holes in the side to see what he could feel. But also at the bottom of the box were two lovely gnarly, very old conkers.

'Cor,' said Stewart, cause it was his best ever find - ancient rock-hard conkers which he could take to school. He would be a champion.

It took a long time to get holes in them. First he asked Portly Paul to do it. Portly Paul bashed them with a nail. If you bash a hole through a conker with a nail you might split it, but these ones were so old and hard they split the nail instead. Then Stewart went to Stringy Simon. He had an electric drill, and he selected a very thin and sharp pokey thing, or *drill-bit*, and whizzed it carefully at the heart of the first conker. Normally when your dad drills your conkers for you it goes straight through and makes a hole in the table, but Stewart's two were stone-hard, and Stringy Simon had to concentrate for a long time, like a dentist at a rhino's tooth.

But at last they were done and threaded, and the next day Stewart took them into school and blasted all the shiny new specimens to fragments, and by home-time he had a one-hundred-and-twenty-sevener. He was the school champ.

The same week that Stewart smashed the rival conkers to smitherines, a strange thing happened. Instead of going down to the park after school the kids from Down-By-The-Traffic-Lights started hanging round the gate. Of Halfway-Up-The-Hill. Not just after school cither, but right smack bang in the middle of the day. And swinging on it, so George had to oil the hinges and chase them off.

Their school was closed.

'It's not fair,' said Lucy Baggage. George wasn't very good-tempered. He swung the gate too and fro checking it for damage. He hadn't had lunch. 'How come they're off and we still have to stay here all day? Holidays ought to be the same.'

'They're NUTS,' grumbled George. He couldn't work the padlock. They'd stuffed chewy down the keyhole.

'We're just as nutty as them,' whined Lucy, making her eye-balls go in different directions to prove it. 'Why can't we stay off school too?'

'Not you,' said George, kicking it. It dropped back in place with a clank. 'Your teachers.'

This was the most George had ever said in one day, and Lucy was encouraged.

'All teachers are nuts,' she said. 'Look at Mrs Greenway. She stirs her tea with a pencil.'

'She marks the books in green.'

'She used lipstick on the white-board.'

'She's a couple of sandwiches short of a picnic.'

They all joined in.

'No, not like that,' George grunted. He was poking at it with a stick now. The chewy was going further in. 'They're in the N.U.T. The teachers' union. They've gone on strike.'

'Lucky devils....' said Lucy. It was quiet for a minute while they twiddled Down-By-The-Traffic-Lights' lucky break round in their minds. 'Why aren't our teachers in the NUT then? Can't they go on strike?'

'They must be in HAMMA.' said George. 'That stands for Hassistant Masters and Mistresses Association. Or maybe they're in NAS, the National Association of Schoolmasters. Or PAT.'

'My mum's called Pat....'

'Professional Association of Teachers. BUGGER.'

'What's that stand for?'

'Broke my stick in the lock. I'll have to fetch the hacksaw now. Clear off to your classes and let a bloke get on with his work.'

* * * * *

It wasn't long before word got round that Stewart was the Halfway-Up-The-Hill conker champ with his unbeatable hundred and twenty-sevener, and that was how there came to be a particularly large crowd of kids from Down-By-The-Traffic-Lights School waiting for them to come out at home-time. They had brought their own conker champ to challenge him, and he had a three hundred and three-er.

Now Stewart's iron-hard hundred and twenty-sevener had got such a fearsome reputation in Halfway-Up-The-Hill circles, that no-one dared challenge him anymore and he hadn't had a conker-fight for ages.

It was quite exciting to get a challenge from someone with a decent conker for a change. He was fed-up with easy wins against oners and twoers on shoe-laces in any case.

All self-respecting conker fights begin with a sort of grand chestnut inspection session, where you hold your specimen up for everyone to have a damn good *gander* at, so they can reckon up your chances. This is almost as important as the contest. The experts get to the front for a good old sticky-beak to see if there are any minute cracks in the skin, especially round the string-hole, which is a sure sign of a conker on the way out.

Stewart held his wizened old prize-fighter up for inspection. It looked more like a dried-up prune than a conker, but that didn't put off the expert conker *connoisseurs* at the front of the circle. They could see it would be a tough nut to crack. Now it was the turn of the mighty three hundred and three-er to face inspection.

The proud owner carefully unravelled it from a quite-used hanky as if it was a pearl. But it wasn't. It was a massive, perfectly round unmarked red-brown conker, shiny and liquid looking as if it had just been taken from the soft bed of its case. There were a few admiring ahs from the edges of the circle, 'cause it was so big - it was more like a bannister--knob than a conker - but the hardened know-it-alls at the front kept silent. It didn't look as if it had been in a stiff breeze never mind a fight, and they knew it. It wouldn't have a prayer against Stewarts stone-hard playground-basher.

But they didn't say anything. The *conker* might have looked a bit inexperienced but the *owner* didn't. He'd been in a stiff breeze or two alright. He had a mole on his cheek and fists the size of hams. If you tried to avoid looking at them, you found yourself staring at his mole. If you tried to avoid staring at the mole you found yourself looking at the fists.

Stewart offered him first turn.

With a mighty swing of the arm the Down-By-The-Traffic-Lights Champion brought his egg-sized conker down on Stewart's limply-hanging shineless sample and smashed it to the pavement. There was a gasp. A pavement-smash is the knock-out blow for a conker. Stewart grabbed for it quickly among the legs and inspected it for damage. There was a big chip in the skin, but that wasn't as bad as it seemed, because it was so old and dried-up the skin didn't fit properly anyway. But as he looked closely around the string-hole Stewart spotted something that made his heart thump. There was a hair-line split in the conker itself.

He wound the string more tightly round his fingers this time and gloomily lined up his shot. The great soft liquidy-looking target hung there invitingly, waiting for the blow. He couldn't miss. Normally a target like that would be the signal for one of Stewart's fiercest shots, but with his wounded champion he wasn't sure whether he dared hit too hard. He wasn't too sure which conker might suffer the worst damage.

With a sigh, Stewart swung down. It was a middle-range shot, the kind that might send your opponent's string round his hand once or twice, but it passed with a swish and missed. He had moved his arm.

Now normally if you move your arm the other player gets his go again, but as Stewart went to claim his shot his eye caught sight of the mole on the boy's cheek and he looked away and changed his mind. Besides, Stewart had noticed that the Down-By-The-Traffic-Lights Champ seemed to have a habit of unwinding his conker after a shot and winding it on to his other hand for holding out. This fellow's a real pro, Stewart thought to himself, he gives his hitting arm a rest after each shot. Maybe he's not so steady with his left hand.

And so he held his conker out for the next blow instead, which arrived with a full-on crack that sent it round and round Stewart's hand to the end of the string. The split was widening.

With a heavy heart he took his second go. This time, by making a dummy swing he tricked the Down-By-The-Traffic-Lights Champion into moving his hand too soon, and managed to catch him with a reasonable shot. But by his third swing Stewart's opponent had the range so perfectly that the crack echoed across the road and back and Stewart's string dug deeply into his fingers practically stopping the circulation.

Holding his breath he unravelled it and looked at the damage. Half the skin was gone now, the conker skin as well as Stewart's finger skin, showing the small shrunken bird-skull of a nut inside. And the split had started to open like a winter sore. A couple more blows like that and his little brown mate would be a goner.

Stewart took a deep breath and made up his mind. It was no good just waiting to be smashed to smitherines - he might as well get in a couple of really good shots while he still could, and see if the other boy's conker would crack. Maybe it had suffered some damage already, you can't go round hitting that hard without damaging your own chap as well. But when the Down-By-The-Traffic-Lights Champ had finished changing hands and was ready again, to Stewart's surprise his conker was still perfectly shiny and unmarked.

Right, thought Stewart, we'll see about that, and without warning he brought down a blow that struck with the force of a thunderbolt. The strings caught, and Stewart followed through with such force that the conker was wrenched from his opponent's hand, swung completely round and with a loud tock it cracked against his kneecap and sent him howling out of the ring altogether.

Stewart held up the tangled conkers. It was such an almighty swing he seemed to have got three tangled up instead of two, must have caught hold of somebody else's on the way round. But when they stopped moving, the explanation was plain to see. On the other end of his string the Down-By-The-Traffic-Lights champ had a lead fishing-weight. No wonder he'd been changing hands. He was clobbering with the fishing weight and while Stewart was inspecting the damage he would quickly wind it onto his holding hand and there would be the perfectly untouched conker again. It still hadn't got a mark on it. They were tangled together, Stewart's all knotty and cracked, ready to go at any time, the Down-By-The-Traffic-Lights champ's new and glossy, and the lead fishing-weight dangling somewhere down below.

The boy hobbled back into the middle, muttering threats and snatching for his conker. He wrenched it away. As he did so the lead weight swung free again and in his fear of getting hit a second time the boy dropped it.

The ring of bystanders closed in to get a closer look. Unable to put his weight properly on his bad leg the Down-By-The-Traffic-Lights Champion was forced off-balance and trod on his own conker before he could pick it up.

There was a sort of juicy scrunch, and when he took his foot away the white meaty inside was flattened into the road.

Stewart looked lovingly at his crippled old prize-fighter. It was a four hundred and thirty-er.

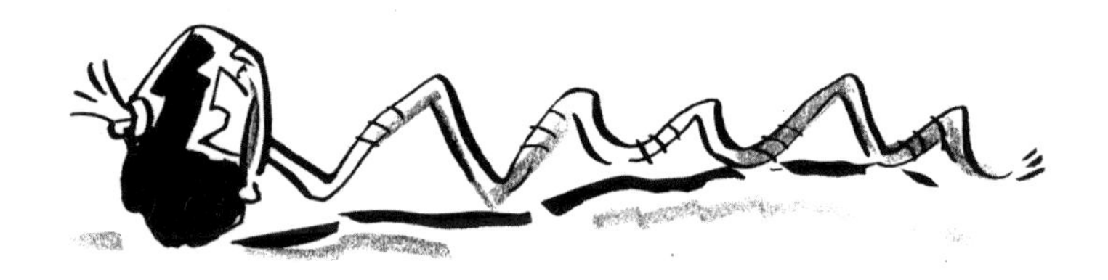

STEWART'S CHRISSIE SURPRISE

[Stewart and the rest go to spend Christmas with his old Aussie teacher, Mr Murdoch, in Sydney, Australia.

They slept for two whole days, and it wasn't until the week-end that Mr Murdoch bounced in and said, 'Right fellas, we thought you might like to get out and see a bit of Sydney today, maybe buy a few pressies for the folks back home. It's Chrissie Eve don't forget.'

The sun scorched through the curtains like an August heatwave.

The big Sydney stores still tried to pretend there was an old-fashioned white Christmas. There were artificial trees with tinsel and fairy lights. They looked as if they were afraid the sun would shrivel them up. There was foam snow in the windows, but the heat melted it and it slid down to the ledges and went brown.

At last Stewart turned round and shrugged:

'It's no good pretending it's Christmas in this weather, it only works in the cold and dark. Let's just go to the beach tomorrow.'

Mr Murdoch took off his floppy hat and scratched his head in amazement.

'Jeez....' he said, 'you're sounding like a true dinky-di already. You're into the Aussie way of life.'

* * * * *

And that was how Stringy Simon, Patsy, Portly Paul, Bertha and Stewart came to celebrate Christmas Day with a coffee, a slice of toast, and a day on Bondi Beach - just like in 'Neighbours'.

As soon as they got there, Trev, Kev, Herbey and Norm got their swimming cossies on and hit the surf. But Stewart wasn't so sure. There was a line of kind of fish-cake things floating across from one side of the bay to the other, fifty or sixty yards out.

'Ah, those,' said Mr Murdoch with a shrug, hardly turning from the barbeque he was setting up, 'they're jest the bits of cork holding up the shark-net... Here, grab that a minute while I wedge another piece of wood under it.'

'Sharks?' said Stewart. His blood ran cold. 'Did you say sharks, or...' But there was no other word it could possibly have been. The surf started to look a lot less interesting.

'You don't want to worry about them, mate.' Mr Murdoch had a piece of steak dangling from his tongs, ready to go on the grill. He looked at the markers holding up the net. 'It's only there for show, no-one's seen a shark here for years...'

Mmm. All the same, Stewart thought, I think I'll stick with the grown-ups for a while, just till I get more used to the idea.

At that very moment, a little creature with a long furry tail scurried from the clump of trees that was sheltering them from the worst of the sun, snatched the dangling piece of steak from Mr Murdoch's tongs and disappeared again.

'Rocky!' gasped Stewart, before he could blink, thinking it was his own pet racoon from America.

'No good mate,' Mr Murdoch said between gritted teeth, 'no-one ever hit a possum with a rock, they move too damn quick. He'll be back, you can be sure of that, and I'll have the little blighter when he comes.'

Now Portly Paul was a bit of a *traditionalist* when it came to Christmas. He didn't very much like the idea of it just passing by like any other day, even a particularly hot one, and unbeknown to the others he had sneaked a Father Christmas outfit into his luggage before they left, and he was determined to use it.

So while the others were all squinting up the tree trying to get a glimpse of the little possum, he nipped off to find somewhere to change into it.

By this time, Stewart had managed to pluck up courage to tiptoe to the water's edge, and Trev, Kev, Herbey and Norm came over to fetch him in.

'Ho, Ho, Ho...' A huge bellowing came from behind, and as they turned round, there was Portly Paul in an enormous great red coat and snow white beard curling down to his belly. It was such a shock, just as Stewart had managed to calm down about being eaten by sharks, that he turned and ran up the beach screaming at the top of his voice. The Murdoch boys thought this was a ripper game and went storming after him, whooping and yelling like barmy.

Portly Paul took off after them, dropping his sack in the sand as he did so. 'STOP!' he shouted. 'It's only me. Don't you recognise me? I'm not some kind of man-eating SHARK, you know.'

Sat up above all the surfers on a kind of tennis umpire's high chair, watching a particularly lovely girl with no top to her bikini, was the lifeguard. The word 'shark' cut into his boobie-watching like a knife and he turned in time to see them all tearing up the beach away from what looked like a large dangerous creature crouching by the water's edge.

Or was it crouching? It was very still. He'd noticed a dog playing in the shallows a bit earlier. Had it been attacked? He wasn't waiting to find out. He blew his whistle like mad. In no time the surf was clear and a thousand screaming swimmers were charging up the beach.

The lifeguard waited for the chaos to die down. This was his chance to make a good impression on the girl in the tiny bikini bottom. He got out of the observation chair and taking only a long pole for his protection, approached the shapeless beast at the water's edge. The crowd held its breath as he braced himself for the attack. He carefully stretched forward, steadied the pole and poked it. It sunk into the folds of skin, and as he drew it back for a second lunge, there, swinging on the end, was Portly Paul's sack.

The crowd laughed like mad. A lifeguard scared of a bag of children's toys. Some of the younger ones cheered. They thought it was a kind of Christmas entertainment. The lifeguard was not amused.

When the fuss had died down and the swimmers were all back ducking and diving in the surf, Portly Paul made his way over and asked very nicely for the return of his sack. He was still dressed in his outfit, though the hat and beard had come off in the panic.

'Oh,' said the lifeguard scowling at him. 'A Pommie. Whad'ya got that Sheila's dress on for? Jeez you're a queer lot over there. Here...' he held the sack out as if it had a disease, 'keep outa harm's way will ya, and if ya want my advice you'll stick to wearin' bloke's clobber while you're over here.'

Portly Paul came back looking a bit sheepish and put the sack down. There wasn't that much in it anyway, just a few puzzles from the toy hospital he'd wrapped up to give out, and they were all squashed now - the boxes had split and the pieces were jumbled together in the bottom.

'Just what I need,' said Mr Murdoch gleefully as he set it down. 'A perfect possum trap, mind if I use it?'

Portly Paul smiled weakly and let him take it. He was sure the real Santa never had to put up with this.

* * * * *

After they'd eaten, the Murdoch boys whooped off down the beach and disappeared into the surf again. As you know, Stewart wasn't too good a swimmer, though he had got his width badge, and the sight of the great white breakers crashing onto the beach wasn't the best encouragement. But luckily Bertha had eased into her swimsuit ready for the plunge, and Stewart decided to go down and join her.

'Want your rubber ring?' said Patsy, looking in her bag. Trouble was, Portly Paul had gone to change out of his Santa suit, Mr Murdoch was rigging up his possum trap, and Patsy and Stringy Simon didn't have enough breath between them to blow a dandelion clock, never mind a rubber ring.

'Look,' said Patsy, spotting a man selling shiny heart-shaped balloons. 'Ask him.' And sure enough, he blew it up from his gas cylinder in a couple of seconds, and didn't charge a cent.

'Ya'd better hang on to her mate,' he said, as Stewart took it back. 'She'll take off right up into the trees if ya let her go.'

He'd never had it filled with gas before. The skin was tight and shiny, and pinged when he flicked it. He was looking forward to a good swim. He found a quiet part where the surf wasn't too rough, and made his way in.

Further out, in the deep water the other side of the net, a school of large blue sharks silently circled its territory. They would glide endlessly up and down the length of the net, nosing and nudging at the mesh, hoping to find a weak place or a hole big enough to get through, so they could have a bite of some of those lovely pink legs that splashed and wriggled just the other side.

But it was no use. The net was made of toughened steel coil and had never been penetrated, and at the bottom it was anchored to the sea-bed with concrete weights. All the same, the sharks continued with their patrol up and down, up and down, never giving up hope of one day having a slap-up five-star dish of fresh, tender human being.

You know how the water in the bath rises when you get in? Well Bertha was in up to her waist, and already the sea had risen by several inches. The line of corks holding up the net disappeared under the surface. The net was strained tight.

She slowly leaned forward, till her huge bosom was immersed, and began to swim. The sea rose higher. A gap appeared between the top of the net and the surface. The corks were straining to close it but the weights held them down.

The largest shark ran his snout along the top of the net for a while, wondering why the mesh stopped. It took him a full five minutes to realise he could poke his nose right over, and swim to the other side. The bathers were at his mercy - he could take his pick.

Not far in front of him was a pair of extremely small wriggly legs, which to a blue shark would amount to no more than a couple of Twiglets, but he thought he'd go over and take a nibble anyway, to get him used to the taste.

They were Stewart's.

Up in the barbeque area, the possum was getting curious. Mr Murdoch had rigged up the sack so the opening was big enough for an average-sized creature to go through, and sure enough, as time passed, it began to wonder if it might be the entrance to an interesting den.

Thinking Mr Murdoch hadn't noticed, it sneaked up to the opening and had a good old sniff. It noticed the bits of puzzle at the bottom.

'Gee,' it thought in its possum way, 'a hoard of *macadamia* nuts. Looks like someone's bin having a chew at them already, I'd better get in while there's still some left.'

Mr Murdoch stayed motionless, waiting for his moment. He wasn't going to move till he was sure it was right in.

At the last moment a sixth sense told Stewart to look round, and there, coming directly for him, was a huge grey triangular fin.

'Help!' he just had time to say, 'shark!' before the jagged mouth opened to take its first bite.

No-one noticed. One false alarm was enough in a day, and besides, the waves rushed in and drowned his tinsy cry. The jaw clamped shut and the razor teeth found their mark.

There was an astounding pop. The gas blasted out of the rubber ring, sending the shark scuttling back over the net and Stewart rocketing out of the water and up the beach with a kind of jet-propelled rasping noise. The force of the escaping gas shot him straight up to the barbeque, where Mr Murdoch was about to pounce on the sack.

The last gush of gas sent Stewart thundering towards him, and with a lurch he pitched head-first into the sack with the startled possum, and the whole shaboot rolled down the hill and into a wattle bush.

'KER-RIPES!' the amazed life-guard said to himself. 'Those pommie guys might dress funny, but they sure know how to do a ripper of a fart....'

And with that he went back to his bikini-watching.

MADAME MURGATROYD'S SECRET NEST

[On holiday in Scotland, Stewart is followed back to the hostel by a little black Scottie dog who has been ill-treated by his owners, and he's allowed to bring him home.]

The old couple next door had a hen. It was a scraggy brown hen with a beady eye and a pink fleshy comb, and it wasn't afraid of anything. It was a kind of wily old hen, it knew things. It had been around.

In the daytime it strutted around its garden, scratching and pecking, gobbling up earwigs and woodlice, and anything else that moved, and at night it roosted in a disused rabbit hutch by the shed. It layed little brown eggs no bigger than a baby's fist, one a day except Sundays which was its day off. The old couple would take it in turns for breakfast - a boiled egg or branflakes. Its name was Madame Murgatroyd.

Another wily old creature of the neighbourhood was Stewart's cat, Batty. Batty had been in one or two scrapes in his time. He'd followed Stewart to school for one thing, and sent a computer crashing to the floor trying to catch the letters on the screen. He'd stalked a postman down the street and had his tail run over by his bike. He was no longer a kitten, was Batty, he was a damn smart street-wise alley-cat. He also had a particularly distinctive tail. Where it was run over there had been a huge great swelling at first, as if a small light bulb was stuck down there - but when that had gone, there was left a kind of flat end which never went down. One of Stewart's ideas was to get the ping-pong table and teach him to sit at the other end and hit the balls back. It didn't work though. He would swish it and twitch it like a true professional, but whenever Stewart passed him a ball he caught it with his paw and tried to bite a hole in it, which is against the rules.

Too bad, said Stewart, you're Batty by name, Batty by nature.

Batty had taken a couple of sharp pecks off Madame Murgatroyd in his younger days, and now they were the best of friends. On warm days Batty would sprawl in the dust where she'd been scratching and let her nuzzle up to him, and there they would lie for hours. Occasionally a fly would unwisely settle on Batty's fur and she would peck at it angrily, and that would be just about the only time either of them moved all afternoon.

So it wasn't any trouble for the old couple to have Batty for a couple of days when the friends went off on their youth hostelling trip - in fact it was Madame Murgatroyd who did all the looking after. The old lady made up a lovely soft basket next to the boiler, but Batty slept in the hutch, and took it in turns to keep Madame Murgatroyd's egg warm. She put down a dish of lovely creamy milk, but Batty shared the water from Madame Murgatroyd's bowl. Only trouble was when he tried to drink it in the same way, tilting his head back and letting it trickle down his throat, it gave him a sneezing fit.

Stewart couldn't wait to get back with Hamish, and introduce him to them. He knew they would all get on like a house on fire.

Unfortunately, Hamish wasn't used to getting on with anybody, he was only used to being hit with a stick and sworn at, and when Stewart put him in the garden for the first time to meet his new friends, he took one look at Madame Murgatroyd and made a mighty charge for her.

There was only one creature lower down than a dog in Hamish's way of seeing things, and that was a grouse. Men might hit dogs, but they shot at grouse with guns, and Hamish had only ever seen them flying through the heather squalking like mad and leaving flurries of feathers behind.

So when Madame Murgatroyd calmly stood her ground and fetched him a large, well-aimed peck through the fence, Hamish *was* miffed. He was the bottom-dog in this place alright, even the grousey thing knew how to fight.

Of course, it was alright for Madame Murgatroyd, she was in her own garden the other side of the fence, and it occurred to Batty he might be wise to show Hamish who was boss on *his* side of the fence, too, before things went any further.

So while Hamish was yapping just out of Madame Murgatroyd's reach, he went up the side of the wheel-barrow, on to the shed, descended on his own side, and took position on the dustbin lid which was his throne and rightful place. He sat in state washing himself until Hamish noticed.

A cat! I'll scare the wits out of it, he thought. It was just the excuse he needed to get him away from Madame Murgatroyd without looking like a coward. He charged the bin and clanged its side with his forepaws. Batty arched his back, but only slightly, as befits a king, and *awaited developments*. It was soon clear that Hamish could only just get his nose over the side of the lid. He yapped a lot, but when it came to it he was too short. Batty carried on washing. When the next charge came he waited for the little black nose to come just level with the rim and gave it a first-class swipe with the flat of his tail.

And so began Hamish's education into who was allowed to do what in the kingdom of the gardens.

Now, as time went on, it came about that there was just one small place in the whole house where Hamish was top dog from the start. And that was the cupboard under the stairs, where Portly Paul kept his ace walking boots. Where Portly Paul's walking boots were, that was Hamish's bedroom. Each night he would snuggle up inside and sleep like a top.

The stair-cupboard was a very unimportant place in Batty's domain, but he thought he ought to just make the point that it *was* still part of it. Hamish didn't have a domain at all, and after a few days he figured he was entitled to one even if it was only small. Each night he would take himself off and tuck down in his furry bed, and each night Batty would follow and try to drive him out again, spitting and hissing, knocking it over, dragging it by the lace. You might think this was a bit mean of Batty, after all it was only one boot - but the thing was, the boot was in the cupboard, and that meant whoever won the war of the boot won the war of the cupboard as well, and that was something Batty knew he couldn't give up without a fight.

It went on for a long time. No matter how much Stewart and the grown-ups tried to separate them they would always find a way to continue.

Just when they were at their wits end to know what to do, a terrible thing happened. Hamish disappeared. They first noticed when they opened the stair-cupboard door one morning. No Hamish. Normally he would bounce out wagging his little stump of a tail and do sprays of pee in excitement. It was as if every day was special - every day he expected to find himself back with the old men and their sticks, and instead the first person he would see would be Stewart, or Patsy, stroking and cuddling him. But this day he was gone. They went all round the house and all round the garden. They asked Batty and Madame Murgatroyd very *distinctly* whether they had seen him. They looked in Madame Murgatroyd's hutch, they looked up and down the street, and in the other gardens. They looked everywhere.

He was gone alright. They looked all day, and the day after, and the day after. Hamish had deserted them.

Funny thing was, Batty and Madame Murgatroyd went mopey, too. They didn't play, they didn't chase butterflies, didn't cluck or meow, didn't do anything much. Actually, Madame Murgatroyd didn't even lay an egg. They were missing him.

'Looks like he's decided to make his way back home,' said Stringy Simon with a sigh one morning after it finally seemed they'd lost him for good.

'But he likes it here,' said Stewart, taking another tea-spoonful of mini-flakes. 'Why would he go back where people hit him and shout at him all the time?'

'*Instinct*,' said Stringy Simon. 'Animals can't help it, they get a yearning to be back where they were born. Maybe he misses the smell of the heather.'

'But we can plant some in the garden, if that's all....' pleaded Stewart.

‘Too late,’ said Stringy Simon, carefully putting a very light smear of marmalade on his finger of toast, ‘he’ll be well on his way now. There’s nothing we can do.’

Stewart shut his eyes for a minute, and tried to see him, but all that came to him was a rainy motorway, with cars whooshing past, and the little black Scottie cowering on the hard shoulder, lost and lonely. It wasn’t very nice.

He had to do something, and so he did the only thing he could think of. He went and bought some small heathers from the garden centre and left them in the hallway for Portly Paul to plant. Portly Paul had been in charge of the garden ever since he’d acquired his ace outdoor boots. Stewart figured that if Hamish hadn’t gone too far, the smell of the heathers might just bring him back. And if not, they would be something to remember him by at least.

It wasn’t long after he’d put them down that he heard the first little whimper.

Stewart sat bolt up and listened. It came again, a funny sound that came from far away and close to at the same time. Hamish? Could it be Hamish?

It was coming from upstairs. Stewart ran up, looking under beds, in wardrobes, behind the toilet. No, it was coming from *down*stairs. He searched the house without finding so much as a whisker. He even looked in the stair cupboard again, which was a bit daft, cause that was the place they’d looked in most of all, already.

Leaving the door open, he stood in the hallway and tried to think where there was left to look. Nowhere. He was defeated. And that very moment was *precisely* when he heard it. Much louder this time, and nearby. There was only one place.

He looked in, right in this time. Before, he’d only opened the door and called, that was all it needed for Hamish to come bouncing out wagging his tail and doing his pees.

But this time Stewart looked deeply in, and waited for his eyes to adjust. There it was again. He looked down, and in a sudden burst of recognition, saw Hamish's bum. He was in his boot alright, stuck head-first down the end. No wonder his whimpers had sounded like they were coming from the inside of a drainpipe. He'd grown so much he'd wedged himself in trying to get comfortable.

'So *that's* where you've been,' said Stewart in exasperation. 'You poor thing...'

It didn't take a jiffy for him to unlace the boot and release him, and he showed his affection by spraying pee all round the hall. Hamish was in the land of the living again.

Stewart wasn't the only one to be excited. Batty went mad as well. Instead of fighting him, he circled round and round, rubbing fur and purring like a maniac. Then they ran outside where Madame Murgatroyd, sensing some thing in the air, had her neck strained right through the fence. Hamish rushed out and planted a great big lick on her - and from then on they were inseparable.

A new bed was made for Hamish in the stair cupboard, and Portly Paul's boots went out in the shed where they should have been all along. There was a patch by the fence where Madame Murgatroyd had scratched so much that she could squeeze through, and the shed became one of their play places.

Funny thing, though, her egg-laying never started up again. It was as if the shock of losing Hamish had affected her workings. And one day, the old man next door leaned over and said to Portly Paul, 'It's the pot for her.'

Stewart begged and begged them to let him have her instead, but it was no dice. A hen that can't lay eggs has served its time.

'But what about Hamish?' said Stewart pleadingly. 'He'll miss her, just when he was happy again...'

'Thought about that,' said Portly Paul, the idea of chicken casserole was already making him *devious*, even though it was next-door's. 'I'll plant the heathers today - take his mind off it.'

It was no use. Madame Murgatroyd was for the pot, and no-one gave a damn. Portly Paul was already getting his boots on in the shed, ready for the dig. Suddenly, a great holler went up from where he was. What do you reckon? Had Madame Murgatroyd sensed what was going on and launched a last-ditch *attack* on him?

Well, she had in a way. When Stewart got outside he was met by the sight of Portly Paul dancing on one leg with a sock-full of egg slime and shell. In his hand the boot was dribbling yolk. Madame Murgatroyd hadn't stopped laying at all, she'd just found a new place - Hamish's special boot. It might have become too small for a bed, but it was perfect for a nest, and Portly Paul had put his great clod-hopper into about a week and a half's supply of eggs.

So, things settled down rather nicely after all: Hamish got a new bed and Madame Murgatroyd missed the pot by the skin of her beak. Portly Paul's skill boots, never quite recovered though. They were cleaned and cleaned, but the smell wouldn't go and they ended up on the next year's guy. And from that day on if ever Stewart wanted to have a little tease he would turn to Portly Paul and say innocently, 'Nice day for a bit of gardening then,' and Portly Paul would look a bit sheepish for a minute, and then say, 'You must be yolking mate.'

THE WILLY ENLARGING ELIXIR

[Stewart gets some help from his old mate Froggie on the high school playing fields, but it's the showers he's really worried about.]

As it happened, by the time Stewart went up to the high school he'd got just about everything he could have asked for. He'd got a walkman, an ace haircut, he could swim, and he'd got a job. He was just about as equipped not to be picked on as you could possibly be.

That was before they had their first rugby lesson with Mr Hughes. Now Mr Hughes came from *Wales*, and his favourite team wore an all-white strip - white shirt, white socks, white shorts - and they were called the Swans. Why do you think Mr Hughes' team were called that? Yes, that's absolutely right, because of their extraordinarily flat feet. And so, to make him feel more at home, he'd got the whole school wearing an all-white playing strip too, and all the boys had to have one.

The first games lesson was a disaster for Stewart. When they lined up at the door in their immaculate white kit Mr Hughes mistook Stewart for a corner post. He carried him out and tried to plant him on the try-line. The biggest boys were put in the *front-row* where they could shove each other and grunt in the rain for the whole lesson. Stewart was told to go out on the wing, only when the ball came to him he found he couldn't fly, and just stood there holding it, not knowing what to do.

'Go for the line, mun, go for the line!' shouted Mr Hughes.

Hmm. *Line*, thought Stewart, tucking the ball under his arm. Now let me see...

It was too late. Stormin' Norman Hogworthy had him. He picked him up and flung him upfield like a javelin.

Actually, it was a good job he did, too. The two front-rows had trundled over to where the ball was and formed a stupendous *ruck*, all tumbling on top of each other until Mr Hughes had to stop the game and untangle them. Imagine Stewart underneath that lot. He wouldn't have seen daylight for weeks.

By half-time the rain was slashing down like bicycle spokes and the pitch was like treacle.

Rain only *invigorated* Mr Hughes, he was on top form. 'Perfect condishuns today boys, I don't want any *shilly* shallyin' now, I want to see some good clean play, second-half.'

They squelched back onto the pitch. They all looked like *tar-babies*, they were that caked in mud. Never mind good clean play. Even Stewart was completely splattered, and he hadn't touched the ball.

He was bursting.

'You'll have to use the *bushes*, dieu,' said Mr Hughes through a bead-curtain of rain. 'We're *restartin*' now.'

Stewart ran for the single leafless bramble he supposed Mr Hughes meant. It looked like rusty wire.

'Rebet,' came a voice. 'Who do you think you are, whizzing on my house?'

'Froggie!' said Stewart, tucking it back in. 'Gosh, you've got bigger. I almost didn't recognise you.'

'Huh,' said Froggie indignantly, 'you want to look at yourself. Who do you think you are, a water-rat?'

'A swan, I think,' said Stewart.

'Hmm,' said Froggie. 'Why aren't you playing with the rest then?'

Stewart looked round. The game was going fine without him. He hung his head.

'I'm not much good really,' he said. 'I never seem to get a touch of the ball.'

'Don't be such a wimp,' said Froggie, 'you're ten times the size of me. How d'you think I get along?'

'It's different for you...' Stewart said, weakly.

'You're too right it's different. If I don't keep my wits about me I get gobbled up. Now stop blabbing and go and knock one of them over. You'll feel much better.'

Stewart looked at him for a long time. He blinked slowly, and did a big froggy swallow.

'I'm going now,' he said. 'That's it. Finished. You won't see me anymore. You're on your own.'

There was a yell from the field. Mr Hughes had spotted him.

'Go on then,' said Froggie, 'pick one out and clobber him.'

Stewart looked round and saw Stormin' Norman. He was big. He looked like a bull hippo after its daily wallow. Stewart looked back, but there was nothing. Froggie had gone. He was on his own.

There was another massive great ruck, and then part of it broke away, making a dash for the line. Stormin' Norman Hogworthy. It was a certain try.

'Tackle him mun, don't just stand there!' yelled Mr Hughes, more out of habit than anything else.

Like a bolt from the blue - or grey, more like - an *impulse* seemed to overcome Stewart, and before he knew it he had launched himself head first at Norman Hogworthy's trundling midriff. There was a gasping thump, and the bellow of a wounded pig. The pair of them lay flattened in the mud like a cow-pat.

Next thing he knew, Stewart was floating above the heads to the changing rooms. Heck, I'm unconscious, he thought, but he wasn't, he was being carried shoulder-high by his team mates.

'Crackin' tackle, dieu,' said Mr Hughes when they got inside. 'You're another *J.P.R.* mun.'

And you're an *M double A.M.H.*, thought Stewart, sliding his school clothes back on over the mud - mad as a March hare. Cor, my head... That's the last blinking tackle I ever do for you.

* * * * *

As a matter of fact, Patsy wasn't quite as impressed with the flying tackle as Mr Hughes had been.

'Look at you,' she said as he took his uniform off after school, 'you need a scraper to get all that mud off, never mind a flannel. Aren't the showers working?'

'Um...'

Stewart hadn't had a shower since he got there, but a feeling came over him things were about to change. If only he didn't have such a tinsy willie, he thought, it wouldn't be so bad. Imagine having to stand next to Stormin' Norman and his great big donger. It'ud be like Little and Large. Laurel and Hardy. Only worse. He looked down at it - it wasn't visible at all at that precise moment, the bath water was so muddy it looked like cocoa. He ran another one. It was nearly cold.

There was no doubt about it, sooner or later he was going to have to...

He was sitting in the religious teacher, Mr Nugent's, lesson the next day, quietly minding his own business, when a note was slipped onto his desk. Without taking his eyes off the board he nonchalantly unfolded it, and had a quick glance down.

'FOR SALE. WILLY ENLARGING ELIXER. GARENTEED. PASS IT ON.'

There was a flash and a distant explosion in his brain. Wow! He looked down again. Yes, there it was, as bright as day. His troubles were over.

A shadow passed across and settled on him. A Mr Nugent shaped shadow.

'Is that a *note* I see, young man. Would you be so kind...'

'Er, pardon...?' stammered Stewart.

'Please sir, haven't you forgotten the *homework*?' came a voice from somewhere else with just a slight edge of panic in it.

'Ah...'

As he half-turned, Stewart stuffed the note in his blazer and swapped it for some pocket-fluff. He held it out.

'Eugh. Put it in the bin, boy.'

* * * * *

Stewart went all round the playground four times before he could find him. Bertie Snodbrolly. He had aspirin bottles full of gunge-coloured paste. Looked like he'd spooned it straight off the rugby field. Talk about a potion.

'Guaranteed to work,' he said. 'Full refund if no improvement in seven days. While stocks last... Thank you, sir. Thank-you...'

It was selling like hot cakes.

'What is it?' said Stewart, looking closely. It seemed to have seeds in it.

'Old family recipe, sir,' said Bertie, 'handed down from father to son. Kindly purchase before inspection.'

It had already cost a homework. Stewart sighed and coughed up his dinner money.

'One application per day, before retiring. Cover with suitable material. Rinse off the following morning. Not to be taken internally.'

'It had better work,' he said.

'Ask my cousin,' said Bertie. 'He invented it. He's got a massive one now, it's damn near as big as an elephant's.'

The lesson buzzer went.

That night Stewart scooped some of the paste out with a lolly-stick and smeared it on. It was disgusting. He'd never smelt such a stink. He wrapped a hanky round it, put his pants back on, and got into bed. His willy was tingling already.

Wow. What if he got a gigantic one. Well, not as big as Bertie's cousin's, you'd trip over it, but one he could sort of *swing* a bit. It would be brilliant.

All night he tossed and turned. His dreams went crazy. Elephants, giraffes, snakes, river eels. Octopuses, storks, geese. Great hanging vines, thicker than your arm. Tarzan. Tarzan of the apes swinging from them. Swinging from tree to tree. Huge, massive great trunks you couldn't get your arms round. Erect. Penetrating the sky, spurting their great canopies of foliage high overhead. Jack - Jack and the beanstalk, huge, never-ending, nosing its way into the clouds, gigantic, FEE FI FO FUM

'HELP!'

Stewart was bolt upright in bed, sweat pouring from him. There was a merciless throbbing pain down below, burning him alive. It felt like he'd cooked it.

Oh no, he thought, in desperation, what shall I do? Um, just a minute... 'Not to be taken internally' No, um... 'Rinse off the following morning...'

Yes, of course. He didn't need a second bidding. He shot to the sink and turned the cold tap full on.

Aaah, that was bliss. It was bigger alright. As the stuff came off he could see it was almost twice its normal size. Bit pink, mind. In fact, almost purple, but bigger, definitely, there was no question about it. Wow. It was worth the pain.

He sprinkled it with cool talc, and leaving his pants off this time he went back across to the bed. Yes, he could feel it, it was swinging. It felt enormous.

Next morning he awoke for the second time to the most excruciating pain. It was throbbing like crazy, making him wince every time. He daredn't even look. He daredn't let anyone else look either. It felt like it had dropped right off. He clutched the blankets when any of them came near. He was petrified.

* * * * *

Doctor Rawalpindi Rajid Kamur Singh Khazi didn't arrive till nearly lunch-time.

'Well, well, well, sir, and what have we got here?' he said, taking a little peep. 'Oh dear, dear, native uprising in the corner of the empire. Very serious indeed sir. And what is the cause of the eruption?'

Very sheepishly, Stewart passed him the bottle. He frowned and looked at it.

'"Willy enlarging elixir". Very interesting. Special prescription.'

He took a sniff.

'Goodness gracious me. It is Indian speciality. Vindaloo. You have put this on your private member's bill? Oh goodness me. With a couple of popodoms and some pilau rice it would be ready for the Maharajah's table.'

'Oh...' Stewart looked at him. 'You mean I've got a curried cock-sparrow?'

'Special recipe sir,' said Doctor Rawalpindi. 'Taj Mahal take-away.'

'But how come it worked?' said Stewart. 'Look, it's twice as big...'

Doctor Rawalpindi shook his head.

'*Swelling* is big sir, but private member exactly as before. Only very small majority.'

'Ow...' said Stewart. 'All that trouble for nothing. Now what am I going to do. It'll never get bigger at this rate.'

There was a silence, while they both looked sympathetically at his poor red, throbbing thing.

Suddenly, Doctor Rawalpindi opened his bag and fumbled inside it. He handed Stewart a magnifying glass.

'See for yourself sir. I think we have first signs of development. Just there...'

Stewart scanned the scene for himself. Yes. Doctor Rawalpindi was right. One tiny, curly little *pubic hair*, all on its own. His first one.

'Wow,' said Stewart. 'I never noticed. If only I hadn't' ve.... Do you think it will survive?'

'One man alone, defying the might of the British Empire,' said Doctor Rawalpindi. He was beginning to get poetic. 'Soon one will be many.'

'You mean, it won't be long before...'

'It is inevitable sir, Independence Day very soon.' He pointed to the tiny whiskery hair. 'We must call him Mahatma Ghandi.'

'Mahatma Ghandi,' said Stewart, leaning back on his pillow with a deep, tranquil sigh. 'Wow... Showers, here I come.'

For details see back page order form.

About the Author

Peter Hayden is the author of Stringy Simon, The Day Trip, The Headmaster's Daughter, The Sneeze & Other Stories, And Smith Must Score..., etc, and founder of Crazy Horse Press/Crazy Horse Kids' Press, which publishes books by teenagers. He was director of the Birmingham Readers & Writers' from 1989 - 91. He has extensive teaching experience, from junior to sixth form. A life long Brighton & Hove Albion fan.

About the Illustrator

Clinton Banbury is a widely published illustrator and cartoonist whose work has featured in National Trust, BBC, English Heritage, O.U.P., Pitkin 'Lookout!' series, and other educational publications. He is responsible for the design and illustration of the Harper-Collins 'Comets' series, and famous for his lightning on-the-spot drawing.

IN-SCHOOL DAYS

with Peter Hayden

PRIMARY

Primary School visits involve talks, readings, workshops, follow-up service (written comment on work done as a result of the visit), and signing session. There is a single fee, no extras, which includes presentation of books to the school library.

All books at signing sessions are well below cover-price.

SECONDARY

The visits involve talks and readings from 'The Day Trip', 'The Headmaster's Daughter' and other writing, including published work by teenagers. Writing workshops are geared towards exam and coursework needs if desired. The one-off fee includes signing session, follow-up service (see primary notes) and presentation of books to the school library.

All books at signing sessions are well below cover-price.

INSET

Talks, demonstrations and workshops from the perspective of the child, teacher, and examiner, with extensive examples of children's work.

'I loved it, I want you to come again.'

'You are a kind person.' *(Yr 3 pupils, Valley Rd. Junior Sch., Sunderland)*

'Best day ever.'

'I wish you worked here.' *(Yr 4 pupils, Bloemfontein Primary, Durham)*

'He's cool.'

'His stories were the best.' *(Yr 8 pupils, Ysgol Llangefni, Anglesey)*

'I think everything was brilliant.' *(Yr 5 pupil, St Godric's Prim., Durham)*

For bookings phone Peter Hayden on 01299 824858,
or e-mail **Crazy Horse** (details page ii)

For illustrator days, contact **Clinton Banbury** on 01277 630421.

NEW FROM CRAZY HORSE...

1. Coming Spring 2000...

The Sneeze & Other Stories

Third title in the Stringy Simon series. This book begins at the beginning, and tells the first seven stories in sequence. Look out for future titles bringing you all the Stringy Simon stories in their proper order.

For details see back page order form.

2. First item from the Stringy Simon present list:

For details see back page order form.

Publications available from Crazy Horse Press

No p&p, delivery by return, order form overleaf:

The Adventures of Stringy Simon - Sampler

'His stories are very interesting, and one day he will get his books published and lots of people will buy them.'

'I liked the story when the two families went to America and met the President, and Rocky Racoon was sent to Stewart.'

'I liked the one about Accrington Stanley winning the Cup, it was really brill.'

'Not as good as Roald Dahl.' (Pupils, 8-12, various schools – *originals available*)

Primary, £4.50 ISBN 1 871870 07 0

And Smith Must Score...

'Lively, readable, eccentric - all the things I like... I recommend it to anyone looking for a good footy read.' *(Nick Hornby)*

'A wonderful, charming and witty dose of escapist fiction... Highly recommended, even for us dour northerners.' *(Derby Co. F.C. fanzine)*

'A football supporter's dream of a book.' *(Middlesbrough F.C. fanzine)*

'In racing parlance it could be said to have been bred by Nick Hornby out of Sue Townsend... It will appeal to all ages from adolescence onwards.'

(Sheffield Utd. fanzine)

Adults & teens, £6.99 ISBN 1 871870 08 9

The Headmaster's Daughter

'We didn't think you were the type who knew about the words snogging, getting-off, or swearing. Me and Donna thought you were the innocent type (speaking-wise)... We thoroughly enjoyed reading it (we are being serious).'

'It's the kind of book that you would be sort of drifting with when you start reading it but when you'd finished you'd read it again because you realise how it fits together and appreciate the detail given at the beginning.'

(Teenage readers - originals available)

Older teens, £5.99 ISBN 1 871870 09 7

The Day Trip

'Gripped by the pace and realism of the writing we join the school outing and are bussed, sailed and decanted onto French soil. From now on, in spite of their luckless teachers, the kids are on their own, our lot rather more than the rest. Lost and late, they board the wrong boat home, merge with another school, and end up on the wrong side of the Watford Gap. Ah - but Mike and Lee have declared their love; and what a day they've all had. Hayden's an invigorating new talent to watch.' *(The Guardian)*

Teens, £3.50 ISBN 0 19 271 510 0

Against The Odds ISBN 1 871870 02 X

George's Mechanical Sledge ISBN 1 871870 03 8

I'm Seeing Stars ISBN 1 871870 01 1

Man's Best Enemy ISBN 1 871870 00 3

Four humorous stories written and illustrated by teenagers.
9-12 yrs., £5.99 - set of four.

The Keeper Looks Like Elvis

[Not really a Crazy Horse production - five football sit-com episodes, each in a staple-bound booklet, featuring a non-league team and their fanzine. Written by Peter Hayden & Robert Pant.]

Adults, £5 set of five.

COMING SOON

The Poppy Factory Takeover

Two humorous verse stories written by teenagers and illustrated by Clinton Banbury.
Teens, £2.99

Uncaging the Word

Creative writing in the classroom - observations and examples from three decades of writing with children.
Adults, £7.50

The Sneeze & Other Stories

Third collection of Stringy Simon stories.
Primary, £4.99

* ALSO AVAILABLE FROM CRAZY HORSE

Flexible 4-colour 'Willy Enlarging Elixir ' key fob.
Suitable for little kids, kids, and great big kids, no ISBN, £1.95 + 40p* p&p
*(p&p does not apply if included in a book order).

ORDER FORM

Complete and send to: **Crazy Horse Press,**
116 Bewdley Road, Stourport, Worcs DY13 8XH.

Please send me the following books by return:

...... copies of 'The Adventures of Stringy Simon' @ £4.50 . . . .= £.........

...... copies of 'The Willy Enlarging Elixir' @ £4.99 . . . .= £.........

...... copies of 'The Headmaster's Daughter' @ £5.99 . . . .= £.........

...... copies of 'The Day Trip' @ £3.50 . . . .= £.........

...... copies of 'And Smith Must Score...' @ £6.99 . . . .= £.........

...... copies of 'The Poppy Factory Takeover'* @ £2.99 . . . .= £.........

...... copies of 'The Sneeze & Other Stories'* @ £4.99 . . . .= £.........

...... copies of 'Uncaging the Word'* @ £7.50 . . . .= £.........

...... sets of 'Against The Odds', &c. @ £5.99 . . . .= £.........

...... sets of 'The Keeper Looks Like Elvis' sit-com @ £5.00 . . . .= £.........

...... **flexi 'Willy Elixir' key fob** @ £1.95 if ordered with books/
£2.35 if ordered separately . . . .= £.........

*[*spring 2000]*

TOTAL [no p&p required] . . . .= £.........

NAME . . . .

ADDRESS . . . .

. . . .

. . . . POSTCODE . . . .

PHONE . . . .

I enclose a cheque payable to Crazy Horse Press for £ . . . .

Signed . . . .